STAR WARS®

ALIENS OF THE GALAXY

written by Jason Fry

studio fun

A READER'S DIGEST COMPANY

White Plains, New York
Montréal, Québec • Bath, United Kingdom

TEEDO

Mysterious scavengers that prowl the wastes of Jakku, Teedos have scaly gray skin, and hands with two fingers and a thumb. Mummy-like wrappings hide the rest of their bodies, protecting them against Jakku's heat. Their coverings conceal an ingenious system of filters and tubes that reclaim most of their bodies' water for recycling.

Teedos are capable mechanics and tinkerers, and have an uncanny gift for finding useful things in the deserts of their homeworld. They are territorial, suspicious of outsiders, and fight fiercely with other scavengers over machinery that can be salvaged for sale. Teedos often ride luggabeasts, cybernetic beasts of burden whose heads are encased in armor plating. The Teedo language is known as Teedospeak.

Increase Your Galactic IQ

Some scholars believe that Teedos evolved on Jakku, adapting as the planet lost its forests and waterways, while others think the species migrated from another star system.

Teedos make no distinction between individuals and the group, and lack names—each is known simply as Teedo. They often seem to know things that happened to other Teedos, even if no one witnessed these events.

Teedos are little, but their spears carry an ion charge and can stun or kill an enemy. Jakku's scavengers treat them with caution, mindful of their unpredictable nature.

TEEDO

LUGGABEAST

CROLUTE

Crolutes are massive slabs of buoyant, gelatinous blubber native to the warm shallow seas of Crul in the Mid Rim. Crolutes are amphibious and can hold their breath for hours at a time, and are surprisingly agile and graceful swimmers. Their ancestors first came ashore during summers on Crul, with bulls fighting for mates and guarding breeding colonies on the beaches. Millions of years later, Crolutes remain a clan-based society ruled by bulls and alpha-cows.

Crolutes adapted to life on land eons ago, but still love the water. Their clan compounds are constructed around lagoons, and no alpha bull or cow's mansion is complete without a deep, lavishly decorated immersion tank. These tanks are favored sites for diplomatic and trade negotiations. Clan leaders debate while floating on their backs, gorging on banquets of gastropods and fermented kelp-ichor prepared by their host's harem of junior spouses and concubines.

Increase Your Galactic IQ

Crolutes are aggressive and ruthless, with clan leaders constantly tested by younger bulls and cows. But actual violence is limited—Crolutes typically settle disputes through ritualized displays of intimidation and dominance.

The Crolute outcast Unkar Plutt became infamous in the Western Reaches as the junkboss of Jakku, seizing control of the planet's trade in equipment scavenged from wrecked warships.

UNKAR PLUTT

DOWUTIN

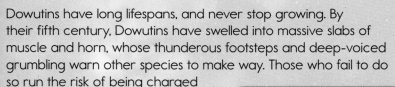

Dowutins are known for their tough hides and ornery dispositions. They evolved from omnivorous herd animals, and their spiked fingers and chin tusks are evolutionary remnants of a time when their ancestors dug up the frozen plains of Dowut in search of tubers, insect nests, and dens of hibernating feeks. Dowutins have poor eyesight but superb hearing and an excellent sense of smell.

Dowutins have long lifespans, and never stop growing. By their fifth century, Dowutins have swelled into massive slabs of muscle and horn, whose thunderous footsteps and deep-voiced grumbling warn other species to make way. Those who fail to do so run the risk of being charged or swatted aside—if they're lucky—as the Dowutin stomps toward his or her destination.

GRUMMGAR

Increase Your Galactic IQ

A hulking Dowutin hunter and mercenary, Grummgar was given a wide berth in Maz's castle.

Dowutins' size and power make them much prized as hired muscle, but few accept such work, viewing most other species as weak, soft beings that no self-respecting Dowutin would serve. Most prefer more solitary pursuits.

The species' homeworld of Dowut is a chilly windswept world with three suns, located in the Core Worlds, near the chaotic boundary of the galaxy's Unknown Regions.

TOYDARIAN

Toydarians spend most of their lives in the air, kept aloft by powerful wings that beat ceaselessly at high speeds. These wings seem too small to keep the pudgy humanoids hovering, but Toydarians weigh surprisingly little. The secret? Their tissues are spongy and filled with buoyant gas that helps keep them aloft.

WATTO

Increase Your Galactic IQ

As Qui-Gon Jinn discovered when trying to use a Jedi mind trick on Watto, Toydarians are tough-minded and can resist suggestion and coercion.

Toydarians find it easy to live with other species, and many have migrated to other galactic worlds.

Toydaria is a foggy, swampy world located on the fringes of space controlled by the Hutts.

GEONOSIAN

The insectoid natives of Geonosis were brilliant engineers, efficient manufacturers, and fierce warriors. Geonosian society was divided into rigid castes, with drones and warriors serving their hive's aristocrats and hidden queen. Few Geonosians dreamed of rising above the caste of their birth.

GEONOSIAN WARRIOR

Increase Your Galactic IQ

Geonosians built battle droid armies for Count Dooku during the Clone Wars, and helped create the prototype of the Death Star.

Geonosian parasites called "brain worms" could animate the husks of dead Geonosians, or possess the brains of living hosts.

After its rise to power, the Empire sterilized Geonosis, leaving the Geonosians all but extinct.

GAMORREAN

Hulking green-skinned brutes with piglike features, Gamorreans are dumb— but also big and strong. Their matriarcho society sees war as glorious, and violent clashes between clans are frequent on their homeworld. Gamorreans are frequently found elsewhere in the galaxy as mercenaries or are hired to serve as muscle for underworld bosses.

GAMORREAN GUARD

Increase Your Galactic IQ

Gamorreans can understand other languages, but find it hard to speak most of them. Their own language sounds like grunts and squeals to non-Gamorreans.

Gamorr, the species' lush homeworld, is located in the Outer Rim near Hutt Space.

Jabba the Hutt employed numerous Gamorreans. The Hutt appreciated the loyalty of his piglike guards and was entertained by their viciousness and stupidity.

WEEQUAY

Hailing from a desert world, Weequays have tough leathery hides and wear their hair in topknots. Resourceful survivors and capable warriors, they often work for Hutt gangs or pirate rings. But Weequays are also found elsewhere in the galaxy, including the ranks of the Jedi Order.

HONDO OHNAKA

Increase Your Galactic IQ

Hondo Ohnaka, the crafty Weequay pirate, became famous (or infamous, depending whom you ask) for his exploits during the final years of the Republic.

Weequays' jawlines are fringed with tough horns that grow as they age.

The species is native to Sriluur, a harsh planet ruled by the Hutts.

HUTT

An ancient, slug-like species, Hutts control large segments of the galaxy's underworld. Their great strength makes them formidable fighters, but Hutts prefer to wield power in more subtle ways. They surround themselves with hired warriors and slaves, and build wealth by controlling illegal business.

Hutts rule a chunk of the Outer Rim, but their influence extends far beyond their home region, known as Hutt Space. Thousands of worlds' criminal enterprises are ultimately controlled—whether people know it or not—by Hutt clans.

Increase Your Galactic IQ

The Hutts' swampy homeworld is Nal Hutta, where the Hutt Grand Council meets to settle disputes among the species' ruthless, competitive clans. Nal Hutta's moon, Nar Shaddaa, is a vast, lawless city-world.

The Hutts have conquered many neighboring planets, turning species such as the Weequays, Klatooinians, Nikto, Vodrans, Jilruans, Sakiyans, and Ganks into slaves or vassals.

Among the most famous Hutts is Jabba, who oversaw his vast criminal empire from a palace on Tatooine. Princess Leia Organa ended Jabba's long career when she strangled the Hutt with the chain he'd used to imprison her.

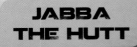

JABBA THE HUTT

DUG

It takes only a single glance to recognize a Dug—these long-snouted aliens walk on their hands and manipulate objects with their upthrust feet, a unique method of locomotion that has fascinated biologists for centuries.

Most Dugs are relentlessly competitive, feuding with siblings and cousins, rival tribes, other species, and anyone else they meet. They have a reputation as bullies, easily offended and ruthless about taking advantage of the slightest weakness. But while Dugs quarrel and fight, they quickly close ranks against outsiders when they need to, putting aside their differences and working together until a threat is eliminated.

SEBULBA

Increase Your Galactic IQ

Dugs are native to Malastare, a Mid Rim planet whose strategic location and fuel reserves made it a battlefield during the Clone Wars.

The strict social hierarchy governing Dugs includes extended families and tribes. Malastare's tribal nations send delegates to the Dug Council, ruled by a doge.

Dugs' agility and astonishing reflexes make them gifted pilots and acrobats. Sebulba was one of the Outer Rim's most celebrated podracers during the last years of the Republic era.

TOGRUTA

Togrutas' red skin, striped horns, and striking facial patterns are remnants of their ancient past—the species evolved as pack hunters, with distinctive markings camouflaging them in the colorful grasslands of their homeworld.

Their horns—properly known as montrals—and head-tails grow as they mature. In adolescence, Togrutas' montrals are mere bumps on the head, and their head-tails extend only slightly past the collarbones. By adulthood, their montrals jut high above the head, and the head-tails can reach below the waist.

SHAAK TI

Increase Your Galactic IQ

A number of Togrutas have served the Jedi Order, including Jedi Master Shaak Ti, Ahsoka Tano, and Ashla.

The Togrutas have colonized several planets, but their homeworld is Shili, in the Expansion Region.

Togrutas are highly social beings, known for being fiercely loyal to their families, friends, and colleagues.

NAUTOLAN

Nautolans are amphibious humanoids with black eyes and thick, fleshy tendrils that emerge from their skulls and drape over their shoulders. Able to breathe both air and water, they are equally at home in either. Their tendrils allow them to sense the emotional state of those nearby, but this sense works far more effectively underwater.

KIT FISTO

Increase Your Galactic IQ

The Nautolan Jedi Kit Fisto fought in the Clone Wars before he was slain by Darth Sidious.

The Nautolan homeworld is Glee Anselm, a green world in the Mid Rim.

Nautolans' native tongue is difficult for other species to pronounce and relies on pheromones to add meaning to conversations.

KEL DOR

Oxygen-rich atmospheres sustain many species in the galaxy, but are deadly poison to Kel Dors. The species evolved to breathe helium and Dorin gas on their homeworld. When traveling in oxygenated environments, they wear breath masks over their nasal passages and mouths and use protective eye coverings. Kel Dors have tough hides, and can survive exposure to vacuum for longer periods than most species. During the final years of the Republic, the Kel Dor Plo Koon served on the Jedi Council, becoming known as an excellent pilot, general, and negotiator.

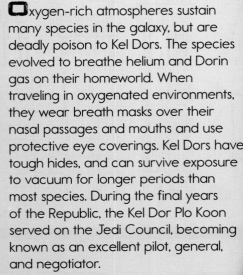

PLO KOON

Increase Your Galactic IQ

Kel Dors are native to Dorin, a planet in the Expansion Region of the galaxy.

A Kel Dor's voice doesn't travel far in oxygen-rich environments, so each breath mask contains an amplifier.

Plo Koon discovered Ahsoka Tano's Force sensitivity when she was a child, and brought her to the Jedi Temple on Coruscant for training.

MON CALAMARI

Often hailed as the soul of the Rebel Alliance, the Mon Calamari are an amphibious species with webbed hands and feet, and fishlike eyes. The Mon Calamari are skilled starship designers and manufacturers. A Mon Calamari engineer brought the B-wing fighter to the Rebel Alliance, and other Mon Calamari supplied the rebels with the species' distinctive, bulbous capital ships.

During the Clone Wars, Separatists encouraged Mon Cala's other native species, the Quarren, to rise up against the planet's Mon Calamari king. The brief civil war was followed by renewed friendship between the two species, but the Empire brutally subjugated Mon Cala as punishment for its rebel sympathies.

GIAL ACKBAR

Increase Your Galactic IQ

Located on the far edge of the Outer Rim, Mon Cala was a key rebel world during the Alliance's fight against the Empire.

A legendary Mon Calamari leader, Ackbar fought in the Clone Wars, the Galactic Civil War, and the Resistance's struggle against the First Order.

Mon Calamari's mouths and chins are fringed with barbels that grow with age, making elderly members of the species look bearded.

MELITTO

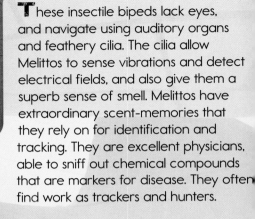

These insectile bipeds lack eyes, and navigate using auditory organs and feathery cilia. The cilia allow Melittos to sense vibrations and detect electrical fields, and also give them a superb sense of smell. Melittos have extraordinary scent-memories that they rely on for identification and tracking. They are excellent physicians, able to sniff out chemical compounds that are markers for disease. They often find work as trackers and hunters.

Melittos live in hives ruled by queens. When a hive grows too large to operate efficiently, several adolescent females—known as myrmitrices—strike out on their own with warrior followers, battling until the victor becomes a new queen and founds a hive of her own. Male warriors who survive the defeat of their myrmitrix become hiveless outcasts, known as ronin. Most Melittos encountered in the galaxy are ronin.

Increase Your Galactic IQ

Melittos are native to Li-Toran, a gloomy and stormy planet in the Inner Rim. Colonies of Melittos are found on several neighboring worlds.

The Melitto ronin Sarco Plank lived on Devaron, working as a tomb raider, jungle guide, and bounty hunter. Plank dueled a young Luke Skywalker at the Temple of Eedit.

Melittos who leave their homeworlds wear breathing gear and carry dispensers filled with sugary nutrient fluid that they use as food.

SULLUSTAN

Frequently encountered in the galaxy, Sullustans have dark eyes, big ears, and distinctive dewlaps. They are a gregarious and good-humored species finding employment as free traders, entrepreneurs, pilots, and navigators. Sullustan ancestors evolved in caves, and the species has keen hearing, superb low-light vision, and a strong sense of direction.

NIEN NUNB

Increase Your Galactic IQ

Sullust is a volcanic world in the Outer Rim largely controlled by the Imperial-aligned SoroSuub Corporation.

The Sullustan smuggler Nien Nunb served as Lando Calrissian's copilot at the Battle of Endor.

Sullustans find it difficult to speak Basic. Most prefer to converse in their own language, Sullustese.

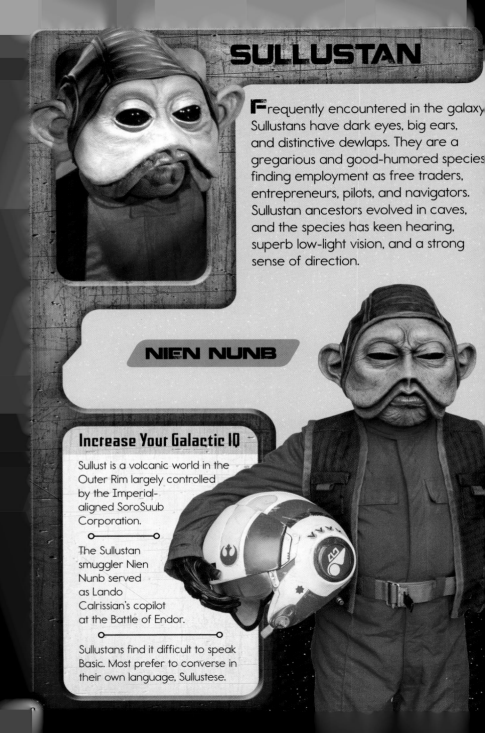

EWOK

Ewoks may look cuddly, but they're fierce warriors, as the Empire's stormtroopers discovered. Ewoks dwell in wooden villages high in the treetops of Endor's forest moon, living in harmony with the animals of the forest. While their technology is primitive, Ewoks are cunning and adaptable, and they know every meter of the forests they call home.

WICKET WYSTRI WARRICK

Increase Your Galactic IQ

Ewoks dwell on the forest moon of Endor, a remote world on the edge of civilized space in the Outer Rim.

Ewok tribes are led by a chief, whose rule is guided by shamans.

Ewoks have poor vision, but their sense of smell is far superior to a human's.

NEIMOIDIAN

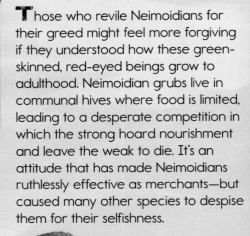

Those who revile Neimoidians for their greed might feel more forgiving if they understood how these green-skinned, red-eyed beings grow to adulthood. Neimoidian grubs live in communal hives where food is limited, leading to a desperate competition in which the strong hoard nourishment and leave the weak to die. It's an attitude that has made Neimoidians ruthlessly effective as merchants—but caused many other species to despise them for their selfishness.

Increase Your Galactic IQ

The Neimoidian homeworld, Neimoidia, is centrally located in the Colonies, near a string of wealthy "purse-worlds" settled by Neimoidians.

Neimoidians fight only when they have to. They prefer to use hired bodyguards or battle droids for protection.

Neimoidians ran the Trade Federation cartel for centuries, and were key supporters of the Separatists in the Clone Wars.

GUNGAN

Amphibious inhabitants of Naboo, Gungans dwell in graceful underwater cities shaped by their clever use of biotechnology. Gungans revere nature and seek to live in harmony with it. They have long, expressive ears, eyestalks, and powerful legs. Gungans speak their own language, called Gunganese, but often communicate using a pidgin tongue that combines Basic with Gunganese words and speech patterns.

JAR JAR BINKS

Increase Your Galactic IQ

The Gungan exile Jar Jar Binks became an unlikely general in the Gungan Grand Army, and later served as a Naboo representative in the Senate.

Gungans share the Mid Rim world of Naboo with human colonists, though the two species have not always been on the best of terms.

Gungans are peace loving but can assemble an army in times of trouble.

LASAT

Lasats are powerful yet agile humanoids. While intimidating in a fight, they are excellent climbers and can move with surprising stealth for their size. Their language is also called Lasat, though many members of the species speak Basic.

The Empire devastated the Lasats' adopted homeworld of Lasan, ruthlessly using disruptors to kill the planet's defenders. A few survivors made their way to the species' original homeworld, hidden within a star cluster in Wild Space.

Increase Your Galactic IQ

The Lasats originated on Lira San, a planet concealed by energy anomalies in an uncharted sector of space. Lira San could only be found by invoking ancient Lasat rituals.

The best Lasat warriors served in the Lasan Honor Guard, wielding unique bo-rifles as ceremonial weapons.

A famed Lasat is Garazeb "Zeb" Orrelios, a former captain of the Honor Guard who fought the Empire on Lothal.

GARAZEB ORRELIOS

RODIAN

green-skinned reptilian species, Rodians have scaly skin, dark eyes, antennae, and fingers that end in suction cups. Their homeworld, Rodia, is a jungle planet whose cities are protected by dome-like environmental shields.

During the Clone Wars, a trade blockade left Rodia facing a famine. When the Republic failed to help, Rodia's senator briefly joined the Separatist cause. Rodians are common sights in the galaxy, having spread to planets from the Core to the Outer Rim.

Increase Your Galactic IQ

Rodian dramas are performed throughout the galaxy, and celebrated for their combination of choreographed violence and powerful emotional storytelling.

A luckless Rodian bounty hunter, Greedo worked for Jabba the Hutt for decades until his hatred for Han Solo led him to make a fatal error.

Rodians see big-game hunting as both a sport and a form of art. Hunters seeking trophies will find many large, dangerous animals—such as the Kwazel Maw—on Rodia.

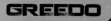

GREEDO

KYUZO

Humanoids with a range of body types, Kyuzos are common sights in the galaxy. Their dense muscle fibers and fast reflexes evolved in the heavy gravity of their homeworld, making them dangerous opponents on planets with standard gravity. Such environments cause respiratory and vision problems for Kyuzos, forcing many to wear highly pressurized breath masks and corrective lenses.

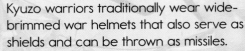

Kyuzo warriors traditionally wear wide-brimmed war helmets that also serve as shields and can be thrown as missiles. Many species seek to hire Kyuzo warriors as mercenaries, law-enforcement personnel, and bounty hunters, knowing that most Kyuzos regard oaths and contracts as unbreakable. But not all Kyuzo are warriors—Kyuzos are found in a number of professions, and many seek simple lives as farmers or merchants.

Increase Your Galactic IQ

The Kyuzo bounty hunter Embo served a number of masters during the Clone Wars. Years later, Zuvio and his cousins served as law enforcement on the desert planet Jakku.

Kyuzos favor their own language, finding the most prevalent language in the galaxy, Basic, difficult to speak and grammatically confusing. Many rely on electronic translators or interpreter droids when speaking with outlanders.

Despite their strong sense of honor, Kyuzos have a fondness for rogues, and many of their myths and stories feature outcast heroes who are forced to oppose the social order.

TUSKEN RAIDER

Tatooine's Tusken Raiders, also known as Sand People, are fearsome savages who dwell in the desert planet's wastes. Territorial and xenophobic, they defend their tribal lands with rifles and deadly axes known as gaderffii. Tusken attacks are particularly feared by others, because the nomads sometimes subjec prisoners to weeks of ritual torture.

Increase Your Galactic IQ

The Sand People regard water as sacred and say it was promised to them by the gods. They think outlanders' use of water is sacrilegious.

Tuskens keep their faces and bodies hidden beneath tattered rags and robes.

Tuskens ride banthas, shaggy beasts of burden that they have domesticated.

JAWA

Jawas are meter-high humanoids whose bodies are concealed by rough-hewn robes. Jawa clans scour Tatooine for discarded junk that they fix up in their mobile, fortresslike sandcrawlers, and sell to farmers and townspeople. Settlers distrust Jawas, who are often dishonest traders, but respect their ingenuity and enormous knowledge about Tatooine.

Increase Your Galactic IQ

Sandcrawlers were brought to Tatooine as mobile mining facilities, but were abandoned when the planet turned out to have few valuable minerals.

Jawa repairs often last just long enough for a sandcrawler to roll away from a sale.

Jawas use handcrafted ion weapons to incapacitate and capture droids.

UMBARAN

Near-humans from a gloomy, shadowy world in the Ghost Nebula, Umbarans have pale bluish skin and colorless eyes that can see in the ultraviolet spectrum. Umbaran society is divided into castes, and Umbarans constantly scheme to improve their social rank. The species' skill at manipulating others has given rise to rumors that Umbarans have the ability to control minds.

SLY MOORE

Increase Your Galactic IQ

Umbara supported the Separatist cause, and the Republic conquest of the planet was one of the bloodiest campaigns of the Clone Wars.

The Umbaran militia's ground vehicles and fighters were more advanced than Republic technology. Many of these craft were seized and studied by Republic and Imperial weapons designers.

The Umbaran Sly Moore was a high-ranking aide to Supreme Chancellor Palpatine.

PAU'AN

Gaunt humanoids with gray skin and jagged teeth, Pau'ans are a long-lived species native to Utapau. While they appear fearsome to outsiders, most Pau'ans are peaceable and friendly— they share their planet harmoniously with the Utai, a diminutive species who performs much of the labor on Utapau.

GRAND INQUISITOR

Increase Your Galactic IQ

The Pau'an Tion Medon served as port administrator of Utapau's Pau City during the Clone Wars.

An Outer Rim world, Utapau was occupied by the Separatists and invaded by Republic troops in one of the final campaigns of the Outer Rim Sieges.

The Empire's feared Grand Inquisitor, slain by Jedi exile Kanan Jarrus, was a Pau'an.

ABEDNEDO

Gregarious and clever, Abednedos are found in professions ranging from freight crewers and soldiers to bureaucrats and slicers. Their skill with languages, curiosity, and easy acceptance of other species have made them common sights in the galaxy.

Abednedos evolved underground, and their ancestors carved out tunnel-dens to create massive cathedrals housing tens of thousands of family units. The species has taken to surface life, and cities now sprawl across the surface of their homeworld, also called Abednedo. These metropolises can strike outlanders as chaotic bristling with ornamental spires, flagpoles, and riotously colored carvings, but Abednedos find them endless sources of amusement and interest.

Increase Your Galactic IQ

Abednedos' dangling mouth tendrils are remnants of sensory organs that helped their ancestors navigate in the darkness of their underground warrens.

○────────────○

After the Battle of Endor, the Empire occupied Abednedo and damaged the planet with a climate-disruption array. Most Abednedos are strong supporters of the New Republic.

○────────────○

Antrot, an Abednedo demolition expert, was part of a rebel team led by Leia Organa during Operation Yellow Moon. Years later, the Abednedo pilot Ello Asty flew an X-wing in the Resistance attack on Starkiller Base.

ELLO ASTY

TWI'LEK

Hailing from the Outer Rim world Ryloth, Twi'leks are notable for tentacles known as lekku that grow from their skulls. Their skin colors cover a spectrum ranging from blue and green to orange and red. Many species regard female Twi'leks as beautiful, and crime lords often force them into slavery. The Twi'lek homeworld was brutalized by the Separatists during the Clone Wars and then subjugated by the Empire, with Twi'lek guerrillas resisting both occupiers.

Increase Your Galactic IQ

Twi'leks' native language incorporates subtle movements of their lekku and is difficult or impossible for outsiders to fully comprehend.

The Separatist occupation badly damaged Ryloth's economy, providing an opening for criminal enterprises. During the era of Imperial rule, the planet was victimized by slavers, and became a site of spice production.

Notable Twi'leks include the Jedi Knight Aayla Secura; Jabba the Hutt's servant Bib Fortuna; and Hera Syndulla, an ace pilot for the early rebel resistance against the Empire.

HERA

BLARINA

Appearances can be deceiving—the diminutive, pudgy Blarina look weak and helpless, but are actually rugged and resourceful beings. Blarina have tough skins and can survive heat, cold, and decompression, and are resistant to poison and disease. These highly social humanoids stick together against bigger species, with allied families forming powerful guilds and mercantile associations.

WOLLIVAN

Increase Your Galactic IQ

Notable Blarina include the hyperspace scout and gambler Wollivan and the Jakku scavenger Naka Iit.

Blarina families are large, and many Blarina have dozens of brothers and sisters. Blarina enjoy confusing outsiders by hiding their true identities and impersonating one another.

The species is native to Rina Major, a planet in the Outer Rim. Their name means "children of Rin."

ITHORIAN

Nicknamed "Hammerheads," Ithorians have mouths on either side of their necks.

They speak a unique stereo language that many other species find beautiful. Though there are notable exceptions, most Ithorians love peace and nature. The forests of their Mid Rim homeworld are famous across the galaxy for their beauty.

MOMAW NADON

Increase Your Galactic IQ

Some Ithorians can "shout" with both mouths loudly enough to stun nearby attackers. This art, known as kougathu, requires training, practice, and discipline.

Ithor, the Ithorian homeworld, is in the Ottega system within the galaxy's Mid Rim region.

Ithorians of note include the bounty-hunter brothers Bulduga and Onca, and the Lothal tavern owner known as Old Jho.

Ottegans are a genetic offshoot of Ithorians, with whom they share the Ottega system. Both species have hammer-shaped heads, but Ottegans lack the twin mouths of their cousins, with a single mouth set low on their neck. Geneticists have argued for millennia about the exact relationship between the two species.

PRASTER OMMLEN

Increase Your Galactic IQ

Ithorians call their cousins *hrumgatha*—"lone mouths"—and joke that Ottegans' physiology means they need to talk twice as much to be heard.

Ottegans and Ithorians live harmoniously on many worlds, and share spiritual traditions.

Praster Ommlen, an Ottegan gunrunner turned spiritual advisor, was a member of Maz Kanata's court on Takodana.

WOOKIEE

These shaggy giants hail from Kashyyyk, a pastoral world of giant trees. Known both for their short tempers and their patient loyalty, Wookiees communicate with growls, snuffles, and roars. Many dismiss them as brutes, but Wookiees are intelligent and technologically sophisticated, creating beautiful vehicles and weapons that gracefully combine natural materials with advanced technology.

One of the last battles of the Clone Wars was fought on Kashyyyk. The Empire treated the Wookiees harshly, enslaving many and using them as forced labor under cruel conditions.

Increase Your Galactic IQ

The signature Wookiee weapon is the bowcaster, which fires a metal quarrel enveloped in energy and has greater range and accuracy than a blaster.

Wookiees are long-lived, showing little signs of advanced age despite the passage of decades.

Force-sensitive Wookiees are rare but exist, and the species shares a deep, almost mystical bond with the multilayered ecosystem of Kashyyyk.

NU-COSIAN

Nu-Cosians are long-necked beings with muscular tails they use for balance and for self-defense if attacked. Like their genetic cousins, the Cosian species, most Nu-Cosians are gentle beings with a love of nature, a sense of wanderlust, and seemingly inexhaustible curiosity. Many Nu-Cosians are encountered as explorers, historians, and researchers.

BOBBAJO

Increase Your Galactic IQ

Nu-Cosians are a genetically engineered offshoot of the Cosians. Both species are found in Cosian Space, a knot of systems in the Deep Core.

Cosian bio-engineers on Cosia created the Nu-Cosians to colonize a nearby planet now known as Cos Secundu.

The Nu-Cosian Bobbajo, nicknamed the Crittermonger, sold animals in Niima Outpost's market on Jakku.

SHIPS OF THE GALAXY

written by Benjamin Harper

A READER'S DIGEST COMPANY

White Plains, New York • Montréal, Québec • Bath, United Kingdom

DROID CONTROL SHIP

Droid Control Ships were gigantic cargo haulers modified in secret to house giant droid armies. The Trade Federation's notorious craft were also modified for battle with approximately 42 deadly quad lasers. These ships carried 6,520 armored assault tanks (AATs), 550 multi-troop

transports (MTTs), 50 landing ships, 1,500 droid starfighters, and a vast army of battle droids.

Giant circular hangars and sensor arrays encircled the command centerspheres. Central control computers designed to radio commands to the massive droid armies from remote locations kept Trade Federation officials in command of battles but far away from any danger.

Increase Your Galactic IQ

▶ Anakin Skywalker destroyed the Droid Control Ship controlling the droids on Naboo by firing a proton torpedo at the main reactor, causing a chain reaction that blew up the ship from the inside.

▶ Jedi Master Qui-Gon Jinn and his apprentice Obi-Wan Kenobi boarded the Droid Control Ship above Naboo while attempting to halt the Trade Federation's blockade of the planet.

▶ Disruption of the Droid Control Ship's signal caused the droids under its command to simply shut down.

43

SITH INFILTRATOR

This devious looking vehicle was Darth Maul's personal starship, used to carry out dark missions for his Sith Master. The Sith Infiltrator was particularly dastardly because it included a cloaking device, allowing it to disappear from any tracking systems and slip by unnoticed.

The ship was secretly modified to enhance its abilities. It had six deadly laser cannons—four were included in its original design, and two were added at a later date. The Sith Infiltrator's experimental ion engines required radiator fins on the ship's wings to be open during flight to expel heat.

Increase Your Galactic IQ

- Darth Maul used the Sith Infiltrator to track Queen Amidala to Tatooine. There he released sinister probe droids that scattered to various settlements to seek out the Queen.

- Darth Maul kept a speeder bike aboard the Sith Infiltrator for traveling short distances from the ship in a hurry.

- Maximum speed: 1,180 kilometers per hour (kph)

QUEEN AMIDALA'S
ROYAL STARSHIP

This unique craft was designed by the Theed Palace Space Vessel Engineering Corps, with a gleaming chromium surface to signify the presence of royalty. Engaged primarily to escort the Queen around Naboo, the glimmering starship also flew on official off-world business.

The frame was designed on Naboo but the sublight and hyperdrive engines were Nubian. The Naboo were a peaceful people, and the Royal Starship was constructed without any weapons. It was equipped, however, with deflector shields in case of attack.

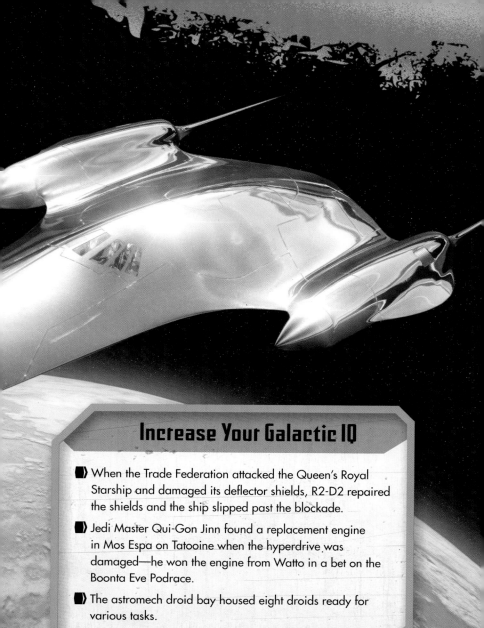

Increase Your Galactic IQ

- ⬤〉When the Trade Federation attacked the Queen's Royal Starship and damaged its deflector shields, R2-D2 repaired the shields and the ship slipped past the blockade.

- ⬤〉Jedi Master Qui-Gon Jinn found a replacement engine in Mos Espa on Tatooine when the hyperdrive was damaged—he won the engine from Watto in a bet on the Boonta Eve Podrace.

- ⬤〉The astromech droid bay housed eight droids ready for various tasks.

- ⬤〉Length: 76 meters

NABOO N-1 STARFIGHTER

Theed Palace Space Vessel Engineering Corps created this sleek, shimmering fighter for the Royal Naboo Security Forces. The design complemented the elegant Royal Starship, complete with buffed chromium finishes on its forward surfaces.

Used as an escort for the ruling monarch of Naboo, this single-pilot craft had a central rat-tail that acted as a power charger, receiving energy from generators when not in use. The ship possessed two laser cannons and proton torpedoes, and two outer finials that served as heat sinks for the engines.

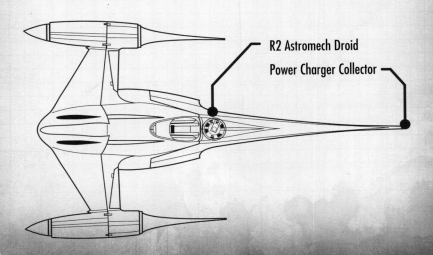

R2 Astromech Droid

Power Charger Collector

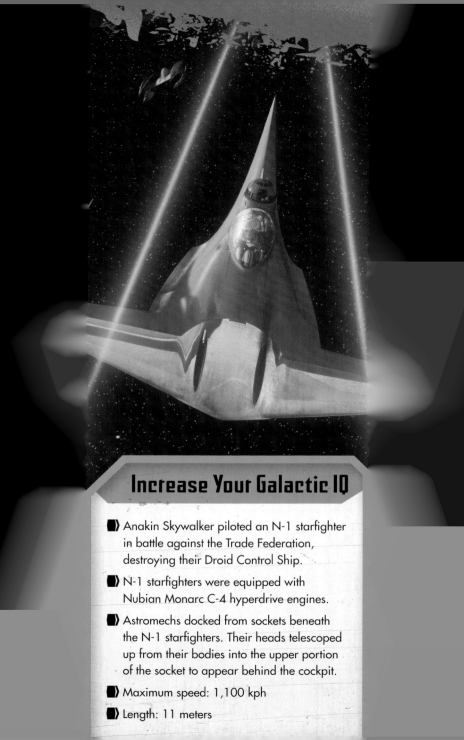

Increase Your Galactic IQ

- Anakin Skywalker piloted an N-1 starfighter in battle against the Trade Federation, destroying their Droid Control Ship.

- N-1 starfighters were equipped with Nubian Monarc C-4 hyperdrive engines.

- Astromechs docked from sockets beneath the N-1 starfighters. Their heads telescoped up from their bodies into the upper portion of the socket to appear behind the cockpit.

- Maximum speed: 1,100 kph

- Length: 11 meters

JEDI STARFIGHTER

Designed by Kuat Systems Engineering, the Delta-7 *Aethersprite*-class light interceptor, or Jedi starfighter as it was more commonly called, flew on missions during peaceful times of the Republic. Jedi starfighters were armed with two dual laser cannons, and had room for only one pilot.

Unlike later starfighter models, the wings were too thin to accommodate a full astromech droid. Instead, a modified astromech was hardwired into a socket on the wing. Its dome remained intact but its components plugged directly into the ship's computer. The droid assisted in navigation, damage control, and hyperspace travel coordinates.

Increase Your Galactic IQ

▶ The Jedi starfighter was not built to travel into hyperspace—instead it docked with an external hyperspace ring that acted as an external hyperdrive.

▶ The red color represented diplomatic immunity

▶ Maximum speed: 1,260 kph

REPUBLIC ASSAULT SHIP

As the Separatists were about to claim victory over the Jedi in the arena battle on Geonosis, Master Yoda arrived to save the day—along with the newly acquired clone army of the Republic. Transporting troops from Kamino, where the clones were created and trained, Republic assault ships hovered above Geonosis and unleashed an attack on the unsuspecting Separatists that many consider the beginning of the Clone Wars.

Rothana Heavy Engineering, a subsidiary of Kuat Drive Yards, designed Republic assault ships, or Acclamator-class transgalactic military assault ships. These giant craft boasted 12 quad laser turrets, 24 laser cannons, and 4 missile launchers. Republic assault ships proved invaluable during the Clone Wars, transporting troops to where they were needed most.

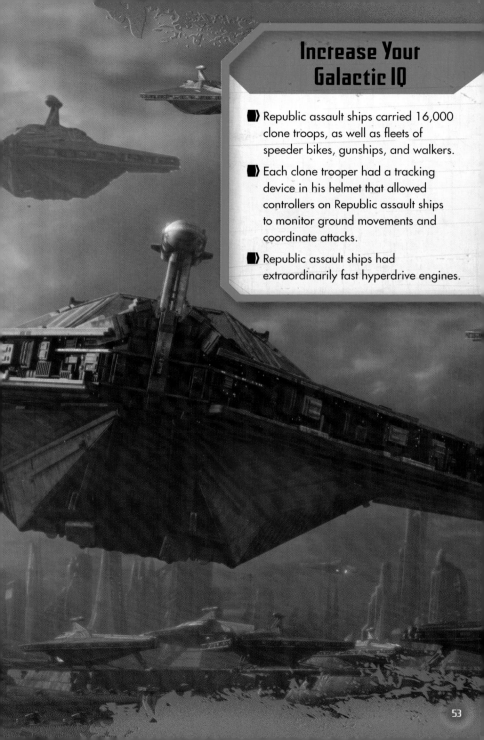

Increase Your Galactic IQ

- Republic assault ships carried 16,000 clone troops, as well as fleets of speeder bikes, gunships, and walkers.

- Each clone trooper had a tracking device in his helmet that allowed controllers on Republic assault ships to monitor ground movements and coordinate attacks.

- Republic assault ships had extraordinarily fast hyperdrive engines.

SOLAR SAILER

Sith Lord and Separatist leader Count Dooku flew across the galaxy in his one-of-a-kind solar sailer, a gift from the Geonosians. The ship was originally a *Punworcca 116*-class sloop, but Count Dooku instructed the Geonosians to add the solar energy–collecting sail so the ship could fly without fuel. Once the sail deployed, the absorbed energy pulled the ship through space at sublight speeds.

The ship contained a hyperdrive as well as back-up repulsor engines. Like other ships of Geonosian design, the solar sailer featured two bow prongs that extended beyond a cockpit orb. An FA-4 pilot droid did the flying while Count Dooku enjoyed his databook library. The luxurious interior featured many ornate decorations.

Increase Your Galactic IQ

- Count Dooku fled from Geonosis in the solar sailer after a standoff with Master Yoda.
- Maximum speed: 1,600 kph
- Sail width: 112.5 meters

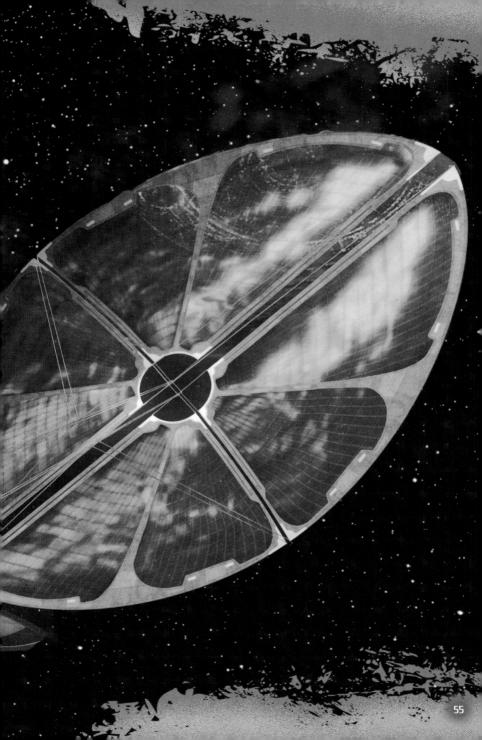

ARC-170 FIGHTER

Created by Incom/Subpro for the Republic, the ARC-170, or Aggressive ReConnaisance fighter, was a multipurpose starship designed for intense battle as well as longer deep-space missions. The wings opened during battle to expose heat sinks and radiators to keep the ship cool. Main laser cannons located on the underside of its outer wings were uncommonly large and powerful.

The craft also had two rear-facing tail cannons as well as proton torpedoes. A crew of three—a pilot, gunner, and copilot—operated the ship, along with an astromech droid.

Increase Your Galactic IQ

■) The Republic used ARC-170 fighters heavily in the Outer Rim sieges, under the command of Generals Obi-Wan Kenobi and Anakin Skywalker.

■) The nose contained long-range sensors and scanners.

■) These ships played an important role in the Battle of Coruscant.

■) Maximum speed: 1,050 kph

TRI-FIGHTER

Deadly space-faring relatives of the Trade Federation's dreaded droideka, Tri-fighter starships were actually pilotless droid fighter craft developed for intense dogfighting and close-range space battles.

These droid starships were equipped with more advanced brains than standard Separatist droid fighters—and therefore were much deadlier. They came armed with four laser cannons and sinister buzz droid missiles.

Increase Your Galactic IQ

▶ Buzz droid missiles did not destroy their target. Instead, they released buzz droids that landed on a target ship and drilled through its hull to dismantle it, leaving the ship adrift in space.

▶ During the Battle of Coruscant, a Tri-fighter launched a buzz droid missile at Obi-Wan Kenobi. Several buzz droids landed on his ship, but Anakin Skywalker and R2-D2 managed to rescue them all from the attack.

INVISIBLE HAND

Massive and terrifying, the *Invisible Hand* played a major role in the Battle of Coruscant. A modified Providence-class carrier/ destroyer, the Separatist Army's flagship hovered above the planet Coruscant, waiting for delivery of the kidnapped Chancellor Palpatine. The Separatists planned on using the Chancellor to win the Clone Wars—but Republic ships intervened and the battle began.

Jedi Knights Obi-Wan Kenobi and Anakin Skywalker landed on board under heavy fire from the Republic, and mounted a desperate mission to rescue the Chancellor before the ship split apart. Once they located the Chancellor, the Jedi fought their way past Count Dooku, countless battle droids and droideka, and General Grievous himself. Anakin Skywalker piloted the damaged front portion of the *Invisible Hand* to safety on the planet's surface, rescuing the Chancellor.

Increase Your Galactic IQ

- The massive ship was armed with 14 quad laser turrets, 34 dual laser cannons, 2 ion cannons, and 102 proton torpedo launchers.

- During the rescue mission, Anakin Skywalker and Obi-Wan Kenobi flew their Jedi interceptors into the main hangar. R2-D2 plugged into the ship's computer and relayed messages to help find the Chancellor.

- Maximum speed: 2,000 kph

- Length: 1,088 meters

JEDI INTERCEPTOR

Faster than its predecessor the *Aethersprite*, the Jedi interceptor was also smaller and more easily maneuverable in battle. Jedi used these small ships to lead their clone troops in battle during the final days of the Clone Wars.

Like earlier Jedi starfighters, these ships had no hyperdrives and relied on external hyperdrive rings to travel in deep space. These craft were also designed with sockets large enough to accommodate a complete astromech droid for navigation and repair assistance.

Increase Your Galactic IQ

❯ Jedi interceptors boasted two dual laser cannons as well as two ion cannons. Unlike standard laser blasts, the ion cannons shot bursts of plasma that caused temporary electrical disruptions to their target upon impact.

❯ Jedi interceptor wings had upper and lower radiator panels, or s-foils, that opened to relieve excessive heat from the ship's engines. These radiator wings were opened primarily during intense fighting.

❯ Maximum speed: 1,500 kph

TANTIVE IV

Owned by the Royal House of Alderaan and commanded by Captain Antilles, the ship flew across the galaxy on diplomatic missions as well as covert operations for the Rebel Alliance. Various symbols and red markings on its outer hull reflected its diplomatic immunity.

The ship carried Princess Leia on many successful missions. But Darth Vader overtook it above Tatooine, after the Empire suspected Princess Leia of aiding the Rebellion with theft of data tapes containing technical readouts for the Death Star.

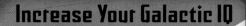

Increase Your Galactic IQ

▶ Although it was designated a diplomatic ship, the *Tantive IV* was armed with six turbolaser cannons.

▶ Soon after it was captured, the *Tantive IV* was destroyed by the Empire.

▶ Maximum speed: 950 kph

Y-WING

Originally designed for close-quarter combat and bombing runs, the Y-wing was the Rebellion's original attack starfighter prior to the introduction of the superior X-wing. Y-wings came equipped with two laser cannons, a rotating ion cannon above the cockpit, and proton torpedo launchers.

The Y-wing was not as easily maneuvered as later rebel fighters, but its durability made sure it was present in all major battles against the Empire.

Increase Your Galactic IQ

- Y-wings fought in the Battle of Yavin, along with X-wings.
- Astromech droid sockets were located behind the cockpit. R2 units helped Y-wing pilots with repairs and other onboard duties.
- Maximum speed: 1,000 kph

TIE ADVANCED x1

The TIE Advanced x1 was a prototype ship that Darth Vader piloted during the Battle of Yavin. Unlike regular TIE fighters, the TIE Advanced x1 contained a hyperdrive engine and a life-support system. It also featured a shield generator, which other fighters in the Imperial fleet lacked.

The ship's wings were covered with high conversion solar panels. The wings' bent design allowed for enhanced maneuverability and speed. The x1 had a more advanced targeting system than a standard TIE fighter, making it deadly—especially when piloted by Darth Vader.

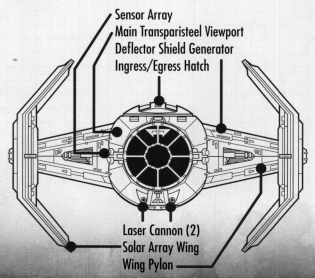

Sensor Array
Main Transparisteel Viewport
Deflector Shield Generator
Ingress/Egress Hatch

Laser Cannon (2)
Solar Array Wing
Wing Pylon

Increase Your Galactic IQ

▶ At the last minute, Han Solo flew the *Millennium Falcon* into the Battle of Yavin, firing a blast that sent Darth Vader's TIE Advanced x1 spiraling out of control.

▶ TIE Advanced x1s proved too expensive for mass production.

▶ The TIE Advanced x1 carried two laser cannons.

▶ Maximum speed: 1,200 kph

SUPER STAR DESTROYER
EXECUTOR

Stationed in space outside the second Death Star during the Battle of Endor, the Super Star Destroyer *Executor* was Darth Vader's command ship and a symbol of the Empire's greed and power in the galaxy.

As part of the Emperor's plan to destroy the rebels during the battle above Endor, the *Executor* was included in an Imperial blockade to keep rebel ships from escaping. But as the battle raged on, a disabled A-wing fighter crashed into the *Executor*'s bridge, causing the Imperial behemoth to spiral out of control and crash into the surface of the Death Star.

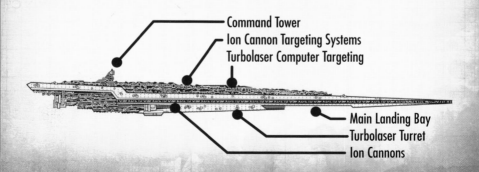

Command Tower
Ion Cannon Targeting Systems
Turbolaser Computer Targeting

Main Landing Bay
Turbolaser Turret
Ion Cannons

Increase Your Galactic IQ

- Admiral Piett was the commanding officer on the bridge of the *Executor* during the Battle of Endor.

- The *Executor* carried a massive Imperial attack force—including TIE fighters and AT-ATs—in its docking bays.

- Length: 19,000 meters

TIE INTERCEPTOR

This ship was created in direct response to the Rebel Alliance's introduction of faster, more effective starships.

Although slightly slower than the Rebellion's A-wing, the TIE interceptor held an advantage in maneuverability due to an ion stream projector that allowed for more complicated flight patterns, such as tight turns. Bent wings gave the ships increased power.

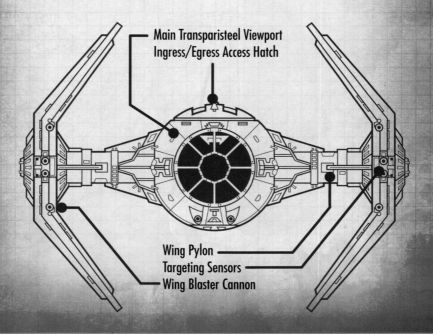

Main Transparisteel Viewport
Ingress/Egress Access Hatch

Wing Pylon
Targeting Sensors
Wing Blaster Cannon

Increase Your Galactic IQ

- Each wing contained two blaster cannons and two targeting sensors, making the TIE interceptor an incredibly accurate fighter.

- By the time of the Battle of Endor, TIE interceptors made up 20% of the Imperial starfighter fleet.

- The Empire planned to replace standard TIE fighters with TIE interceptors.

- Like standard TIE fighters, TIE interceptors did not have life-support systems, hyperdrives, or deflector shields.

A-WING

The A-wing was the fastest starfighter in the rebel fleet, due to two specially designed engines.

These engines contained thrust-vector controls that worked with associated thruster-control jets for maneuverability in battle. To give maximum power to the engines, the ship was designed with weak shield generators and thin armor plating.

Increase Your Galactic IQ

- A-wing controls were extremely sensitive. Only the most experienced pilots could handle these starfighters at top speed.

- A-wings played a huge part in the Rebel Alliance's success during the Battle of Endor.

- A-wings were equipped with two laser cannons.

- Length: 9.6 meters

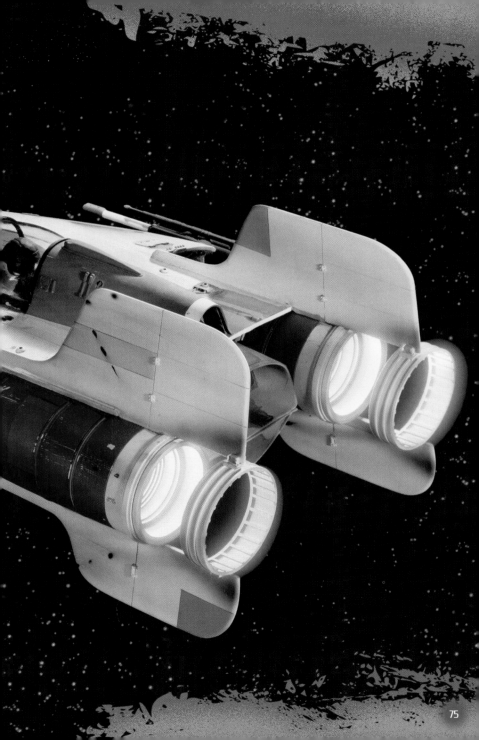

B-WING

The B-wing starfighter was one long wing with a cockpit at one end, and two folding airfoils that opened during flight. Heavily armed, B-wings were deadly in battle. A typical B-wing armament included two auto-blasters on the cockpit, two proton torpedo launchers at the midsection, ion cannons at the tip of each folding wing, and one laser cannon and proton torpedo launcher located at the base of the main wing.

This fighter's most important feature was its cockpit, which was surrounded by a gyrostabilization system that kept the pilot upright, no matter at what angle the ship was flying.

Increase Your Galactic IQ

- ▶ If the gyro surrounding the cockpit suffered damage, the B-wing would spiral out of control.

- ▶ The B-wing was designed so that its standard weaponry could be replaced with custom weapons, depending on its missions.

- ▶ Maximum speed: 950 kph

MON CALAMARI CRUISER

Originally designed for civilian transport, these giant starships were modified for battle when the Mon Calamari donated them to the Rebel Alliance. Modifications made the cruisers especially durable in battle, in particular the overlapping shield generators. If one generator incurred damage, a nearby shield continued to protect the affected area during repairs.

Home One was Admiral Ackbar's command ship and the Alliance's flagship during the Battle of Endor. As the battle raged on, Admiral Ackbar ordered all rebel ships to concentrate fire on Super Star Destroyer *Executor*, ultimately leading to its destruction.

Increase Your Galactic IQ

- ▶ *Home One* had a tractor beam, plus 36 ion cannons and 29 turbolasers.
- ▶ *Home One* housed a massive fleet of 120 starfighters.
- ▶ Length: 1,300 meters